To my father

The illustrations in this book were made with colored pencils.

Library of Congress Cataloging-in-Publication Data
Names: Yum, Hyewon, author, illustrator.
Title: Grandpa across the ocean / Hyewon Yum.
Description: New York, NY : Abrams Books for Young Readers, 2021. |
Summary: When a little boy visits his grandfather on the other side of
the ocean, everything is unfamiliar and boring until time together
proves that Grandpa can be a lot of fun.
Identifiers: LCCN 2020005159 | ISBN 9781419742255 (hardcover)
Subjects: CYAC: Grandfathers--Fiction. | Korea--Fiction.
Classification: LCC PZ7.Y89656 Gr 2021 | DDC [E]--dc23
LC record available at https://lccn.loc.gov/2020005159

Text and illustrations copyright © 2021 Hyewon Yum
Book design by Hana Anouk Nakamura

Printed and bound in China
10 9 8 7 6 5 4 3 2 1

Abrams Books for Young Readers are available at special discounts when purchased in quantity
for premiums and promotions as well as fundraising or educational use. Special editions can also be
created to specification. For details, contact specialsales@abramsbooks.com or the address below.

Abrams® is a registered trademark of Harry N. Abrams, Inc.

ABRAMS The Art of Books
195 Broadway, New York, NY 10007
abramsbooks.com

Grandpa Across the Ocean

HYEWON YUM

ABRAMS BOOKS FOR YOUNG READERS
NEW YORK

My Grandpa lives on the other side of the ocean.

Where Grandpa lives, it smells strange.
It sounds strange.

370

When I say "Hi,"

Grandpa bows.

Then he hugs me like no other person.

I can't quite understand what he says,

and he can't hear me well.

Yuck!

Grandpa eats things I don't want to eat.

Grandpa's house is the most boring place on earth.

There's nothing for me to do.

Humph!

He always watches his TV.

A very important thing is on the news, so I can't watch my cartoon.

And he takes naps all the time in his chair.

My ball is the only toy here.

I kick it in the house.

Until it flies toward Grandpa's orchid pots...

I'm in trouble.

But Grandpa doesn't seem mad at all.

His hands are warm and gentle.

Still, I feel like crying.

So Grandpa quickly fetches me some peaches.

A peach is so sweet, I forget about crying.

Then he takes down his mini car from the very top of the bookshelf.

And he even lets me watch my cartoon.

Grandpa laughs, just like me.

When we go to the market to buy a new flowerpot, everybody says I look just like my grandpa.

Grandpa smiles.

I hold his hand tight.

He teaches me his Korean words,
and I teach him how to say them in English.

생선
fish

수박
watermelon

모자
hat

But with Grandpa, I don't need to say the word for what I want most.

He already knows.

Grandpa likes chocolate best, just like me.

The next day, Grandpa drives me to the beach.
In the car that smells like Grandpa, we listen to Grandpa's songs.

Now they're my songs, too.

He's a great singer, just like me.

"What a wonderful world!"

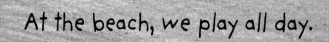

At the beach, we play all day.

I get tired, but Grandpa doesn't seem to.

I have to scold him from time to time.

He's such a troublemaker.

Just like me.

Grandpa doesn't even take a nap.

He's a bit spoiled with me.

He is my grandpa, after all.

We watch the waves come and go.

They look just like the waves on the other side of the ocean.

Now where Grandpa lives, it smells familiar.

It sounds familiar.

And it feels like home.

I can say "Hi" in Grandpa's words.

안녕하세요!

I can eat the kimchi Grandpa likes.

I wish summer would go on forever.

Grandpa agrees.

But we both know I have to go back across the ocean.

When I bow to say goodbye, Grandpa says, "Bye!"

Then he hugs me like
no other person.

Just like Grandpa.

And I can't, can't wait for next summer.